Dear Santa,

Here is what I want for Christmas:

1) New hockey skates—the best ones, please
2) Invader collecting cards—the entire set
   if possible: 1-5,000
3) No clothes!
4) Aquarium like the one in the library, only
   with a piranha in it
5) A canoe for our trip next summer
6) Earplugs to block out my sister's talking,
   which never stops
7) Bicycle with the most gears
8) One large tree fort (in the oak tree)

   Sincerely,

James B. Dobbins

Dear Santa

The Letters of James B. Dobbins

Compiled by
Bill Harley

Pictures drawn by
R.W. Alley

HarperCollinsPublishers

Library of Congress Cataloging-in-Publication Data   Harley, Bill, 1954-   Dear Santa : the letters of James B. Dobbins / compiled by Bill Harley ; pictures drawn by R. W. Alley.— 1st ed.   p.   cm.   Summary: James Dobbins writes letters to Santa Claus, detailing what he and some family members want for Christmas and explaining his behavior of the past year.   ISBN 0-06-623778-5 — ISBN 0-06-623779-3 (lib. bdg.)   [1. Santa Claus—Fiction. 2. Letters—Fiction. 3. Behavior—Fiction.] I. Alley, R. W. (Robert W.) ill. II. Title. PZ7.H22655De 2005   2004022467   [E]—dc22   CIP   AC

Typography by Amelia May Anderson   1 2 3 4 5 6 7 8 9 10
❖   First Edition

In memory of Ruth Wolfe Harley,
my first writing teacher
—B.H.

To Max, whose correspondence with
Santa goes way back
—R.W.A.

December 2

Dear Santa,

After I sent you my Christmas list, I thought of something else. I read about a kid who has a hockey rink in his backyard. I think we might have enough room for one. I just thought I would tell you.

I have been very good this year, as you probably know. I even ate Aunt Marjorie's cranberry stuff at Thanksgiving and I didn't throw up, though I felt like it. And I have not done anything horrible to Jessica, even though she is THE MOST ANNOYING FOUR-YEAR-OLD SISTER ON THE PLANET. If you need another elf, I could ship her up to the North Pole. Let me know.

Sincerely,
James Dobbins

December 5

Dear Santa,
    I am just checking to see how you are coming on my list. Sometimes it helps to be reminded of things, like how good I've been. Do you remember? And please remember that I do not want any clothes. Unless you count a hockey helmet as clothes. If you do, then I'd like clothes, but only if it's a hockey helmet.

            Still sincerely,
            Jim Dobbins

Dear Santa,   December 6

        Maybe I should explain about that
one accident during last spring vacation.
I thought Dad would laugh when the
ketchup came out. I tried to explain why
it was funny, but he didn't get it.

        Sincerely,
        James Dobbins

P.S. I am <u>still</u> being
nice to Jessica.
You have no
idea how hard
that can be.

December 8

Dear Santa,

About school today—I really
don't know why I put those crayons
there. Maybe my brain melted, just
like the crayons did. Mrs. Thompkins
was a little mad, but the janitor fixed
everything. He said not to worry.
Accidents can happen!

Sincerely,
Jim Dobbins

P.S. I'm <u>still</u> still being nice to
Jessica, though. Don't forget that.

December 9

Dear Santa,

Okay, here is the truth about what happened last summer:

* I was only trying to get the paint off of my new shirt. I guess I shouldn't have been wearing it, but I thought that I could open the can of paint without spilling any.

* I didn't want to use hand soap to clean the paint off because my mom said you should never use that to wash clothes. I thought the bubble bath might work.

* When Dad called, I knew I had to see what he wanted.

*   Otherwise, I wouldn't have forgotten, and I would have turned the water off in the bathroom sink.

*   I think if there wasn't a crack in the bathroom tile, it might not have dripped down into the kitchen cupboards.

*   The crackers and the food were probably kind of old and stale anyway, and we would have had to throw them out sooner or later.

*   The cupboards and walls look a lot better with the new paint.

*   The new ceiling is really nice. Even Mom says so.

I can't think of anything else I've done that you should know about.

Still sincerely again,
Jim Dobbins

December 11

Dear Santa,

   I know I said I didn't want any clothes, but if you have to bring some, I would like SEVEN RIGHT-HAND GLOVES. I have all the left-hand ones under my bed, and I can't tell my mom I lost another or she will lose her mind. She says she's already lost it six times, but I think this time she really might.

   With great concern,
   Jimmy Dobbins
P.S. I am still being nice to Jessica almost all the time.

December 13

Dear Santa,

I was only imitating the Statue of Liberty. Mrs. Thompkins told me she didn't care if I was George Washington, I still wasn't allowed to stand on top of my desk.

With apologies,
Jimmy Dobbins

December 14

Dear Santa,

I am still looking for Harry. I have lost hamsters before, and they have always come back. I hope I find him before Dad does.

With great respect,
Jimmy Dobbins

P.S. My mom asked what we should give Mrs. Thompkins. I heard her say she needed some aspirin. What do you think?

December 15

Dear Santa,

I only wanted to see how the computer worked.
And the phone.
And the garage door opener.

Sorry again,
Jimmy

P.S. I am making Mrs. Thompkins a pencil holder. She is always losing her pencils.

ERROR

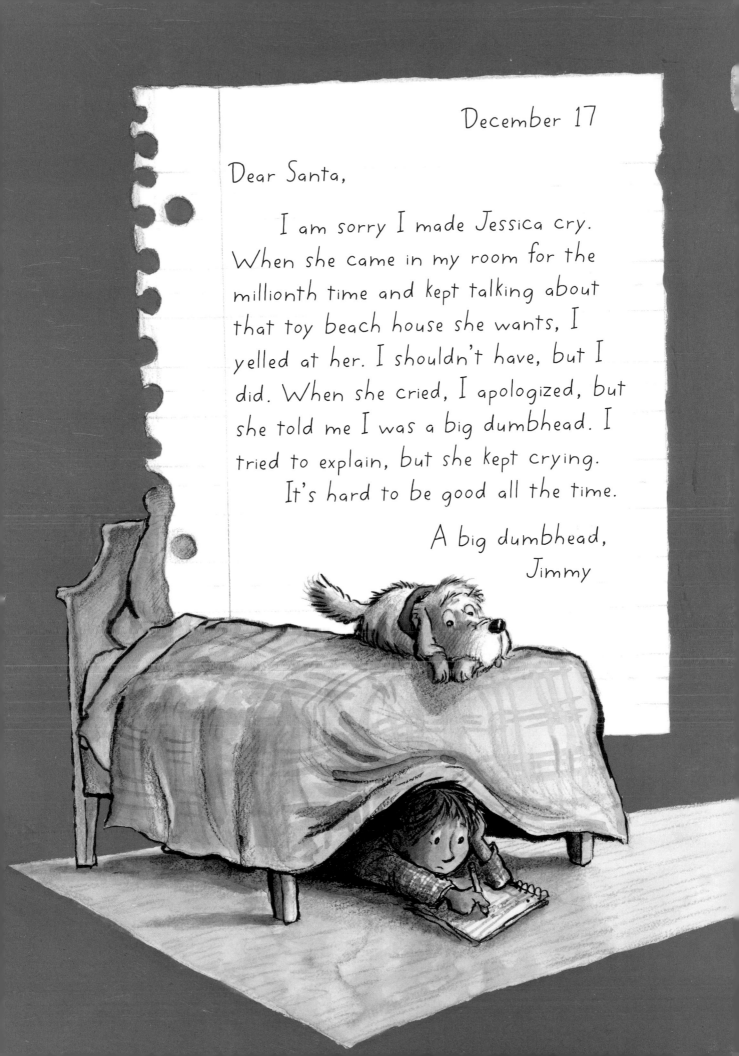

December 17

Dear Santa,

I am sorry I made Jessica cry. When she came in my room for the millionth time and kept talking about that toy beach house she wants, I yelled at her. I shouldn't have, but I did. When she cried, I apologized, but she told me I was a big dumbhead. I tried to explain, but she kept crying.

It's hard to be good all the time.

A big dumbhead,
Jimmy

FOUR DAYS TO GO!

Dear Santa,

You have a great job. You should have seen Mrs. Thompkins's face when she opened the present. She got three other pencil holders, so maybe it was the note I wrote her that made her laugh. She also gave me a hug. It felt pretty good. Do you ever get to watch people open presents? If I were you, I would hang around a little longer. It's the best part.

Jimmy

P.S. My dad looked at me like I was crazy when I mentioned I wanted a hockey rink. He asked me if I wanted a Zamboni, too. Do you think he was joking?

THREE DAYS AND COUNTING

Dear Santa,

If you were going to bring Mom those slippers with the green toes she really likes, you can cross that off your list. Dad had to lend me five dollars, but I got them!

Maybe when you come, you could look for Harry, too. I think he's in my parents' room.

If I could, I would give Tommy Eldredge a dog. He misses Ralph, even though he smelled bad. Maybe you could get Tommy one that doesn't smell so bad.

Your assistant,
Jimmy Dobbins

TWO DAYS LEFT!!!
NEWS FLASH!!!

Dear Santa,
Don't look for Harry. We found him. He had babies. He is a she. My dad is calling her Harriet. My mom is not happy, but I am.
Eagerly awaiting your arrival,
Jimmy

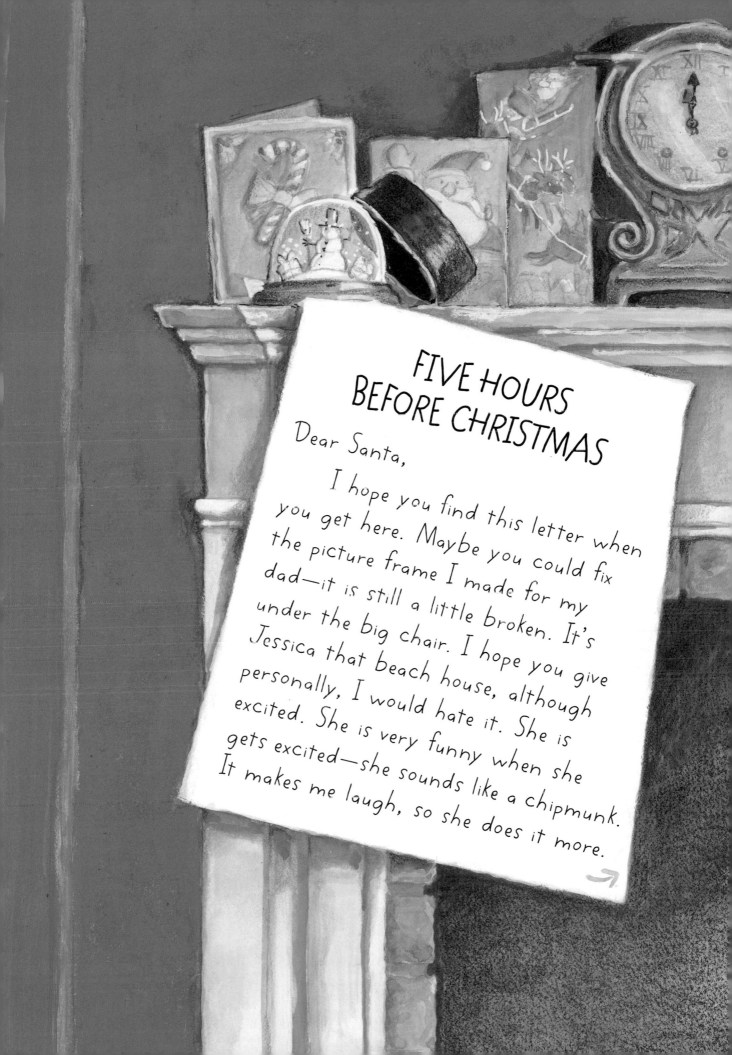

FIVE HOURS
BEFORE CHRISTMAS

Dear Santa,

I hope you find this letter when you get here. Maybe you could fix the picture frame I made for my dad—it is still a little broken. It's under the big chair. I hope you give Jessica that beach house, although personally, I would hate it. She is excited. She is very funny when she gets excited—she sounds like a chipmunk. It makes me laugh, so she does it more.

I was thinking that new skates and one hockey stick are all I really want. Don't worry about the other stuff. I'm probably not sleeping if you want to say hi. I'm the second door down the hall. Don't wake Jessica—she's in the first room.

I left orange ice pops in the freezer for the reindeer. I figured they would be sick of carrots. I left you something too, but it's not food. It's a hockey puck.

Merry Christmas, Santa.

Your old pal,
Jimmy